ᑭᓯᒥ ᑕᐃᒪᐃᕙᒃᑐᑦ ᐊᖕᒥᕐᖁᓂᔭᕐᓂ

ᑭᓯᒥ ᑕᐃᒪ⁻⁻ᐸᖅ ᑐᖔ

ᐊᕐᓇ ᑯ ᓗᒃ ᑫᓕᓴᓐ
ᑎᑎᕋᐅᔭᖅᑐᖅ
ᐃᐱᒃᓴᐅᑦ ᑫᓕᓴᓐ

Arnakuluk Vuriisan
Titiraujaqtuq
Ipiksaut Vuriisan

Angnakuluk Friesen
Pictures by
Ippiksaut Friesen

ᐃᓄᒃᑎᑐᓕᕆᔪᖅ ᔨᓐ ᑯᓱᒐᖅ
Inuktituulirijuq Jiin Kusugaq
Translated by Jean Kusugak

Kisimi Taimaippaktut Angirrarijarani

ᐊᖅᑎᕆᖅᕋᓯᖅᑎ

Only in My Hometown

GROUNDWOOD BOOKS
HOUSE OF ANANSI PRESS
TORONTO   BERKELEY

Published in Canada and the USA in 2017 by Groundwood Books

Groundwood Books / House of Anansi Press
groundwoodbooks.com

We acknowledge for their financial support of our publishing program the
Canada Council for the Arts, the Ontario Arts Council and the Government
of Canada.

Canada Council Conseil des Arts
for the Arts du Canada

ONTARIO ARTS COUNCIL
CONSEIL DES ARTS DE L'ONTARIO
an Ontario government agency
un organisme du gouvernement de l'Ontario

With the participation of the Government of Canada
Avec la participation du gouvernement du Canada | Canadä

Library and Archives Canada Cataloguing in Publication

Friesen, Angnakuluk, author
     Kisimi taimaippaktut angirrarijarani / Arnakuluk Vuriisan ; titiraujaqtuq,
Ipiksaut Vuriisan ; inuktituulirijuq, Jiin Kusugaq = Only in my hometown
/ Angnakuluk Friesen ; pictures by Ippiksaut Friesen ; translated by Jean
Kusugak.

Text in Inuktitut (romanized and syllabic characters) and English.
Translated from the original English.
Issued in print and electronic formats.
ISBN 978-1-55498-883-9 (hardcover). — ISBN 978-1-55498-884-6 (PDF)

     I. Friesen, Ippiksaut, illustrator II. Kusugak, Jean, translator III. Friesen,
Angnakuluk. Only in my hometown. IV. Friesen, Angnakuluk. Only in my
hometown. Inuktitut. V. Title. VI. Title: Only in my hometown.

PS8611.R534O54155 2017   jC813'.6   C2016-908199-0
C2017-901154-5

This book was written in English and translated into Inuktitut (the Aivilik
dialect). The Inuktitut language is represented in two forms — syllabics and
transliterated roman orthography. The publisher would like to thank Nellie T.
Kusugak for kindly proofreading the Inuktitut text.

The illustrations were painted with watercolor and acrylic on elephant poo
paper, then composited digitally.
Design by Michael Solomon
Printed and bound in Malaysia

MIX
Paper from
responsible sources
FSC
www.fsc.org   FSC® C012700

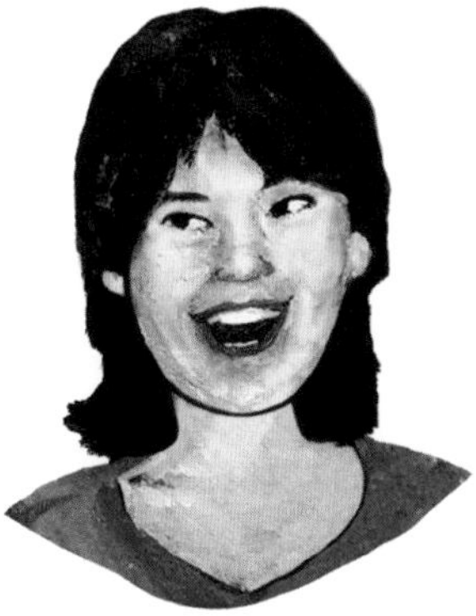

ᐊᕐᓇᕐᕕᒐᓄᑦ ᑖᓇᒧᑦ, ᓇᒡᓕᒍᑦᑕᐅᓚᐅᕐᒪᑦ
ᓇᒡᓕᒋᔭᐅᔪᒻᒪᕆᐊᓘᓚᐅᖅᖢᓂᓗ. ᐃᓚᒃᑲᓄᑦ
ᑯᓱᒐᒃᑯᓐᓄᑦ ᑲᖏᖅᖢᓂᕐᒥᐅᑕᐅᑎᓪᓗᖓ
ᑕᒫᓃᑦᑕᕆᐊᕐᑲᕐᓂᕋ ᑐᑭᓯᓇᖅᓯᑎᓯᒪᖕᒪᒍ. ᑕᒪᓐᓇ
ᑐᕌᖕᒐᑎᑕᕋᑦᑕᐅᖅ ᐊᒥᓲᔪᓄᑦ ᐊᓯᐅᓯᒪᔪᓄᑦ
ᐃᓄᐊᖅᑕᐅᓯᒪᔪᓄᓪᓗ ᓄᓇᕐᑲᖅᑳᖅᓯᒪᔪᓄᑦ ᐊᕐᓇᕐᓄᑦ
ᓂᕕᐊᖅᓵᑯᓗᖕᓄᑦ ᐃᓚᒋᔭᖏᓐᓄᓪᓗ.
— ᐊᕐᓇᑯᓗᒃ ᕗᕇᓴᓐ

ᐊᖕᒐᔪᒐᓄᑦ ᐊᕐᓇᑯᓗᖕᒧᑦ ᐊᒻᒪᓗ ᐊᕐᓇᕐᕕᒃᑲᓄᑦ.
— ᐃᐱᒃᓴᐅᑦ ᕗᕇᓴᓐ

Arnarviganut Taanamut, nagliguttaulaurmat
nagligijaujummarialuulauqłunilu. Ilakkanut
Kusugakkunnut Kangiqłinirmiutautillunga
tamaaniittariaqarnira tukisinaqsitisimangmagu.
Tamanna turaangatitarattauq amisuujunut asiusimajunut
inuaqtausimajunullu nunaqaqqaaqsimajunut arnarnut
niviaqsaakulungnut ilagijanginnullu.
— Arnakuluk Vuriisan

Angajuganut Arnakulungmut ammalu
arnarvikkanut.
— Ipiksaut Vuriisan

To my auntie Donna, who loved and was loved so fiercely.
To my Kusugak family who make my life in Kangiqłiniq
meaningful. To the many other missing and murdered
Indigenous women and girls and their families.
— Angnakuluk Friesen

To my sister Angnakuluk and to my aunties.
— Ippiksaut Friesen

ᐃᒃᓯᕙᐳᖢᖓ ᐊᑕᐸᖖᒍᐊᕌᓗᖕᒥ
ᐃᖅᑲᐅᒪᐃᓐᓇᖅᖢᖓ ᐊᓈᓇᒪ ᐅᖃᖃᑦᑕᖅᑕᖓᓂᒃ.

Iksivablunga alipannguaraalungmi
iqqaumainnaqłunga anaanama uqaqattaqtanganik.

Sitting on the elephant,
always remembering what my mom said.

"ᑕᐅᐁᓂ ᖅᐊᖅᑲᑦᑖᖕᒌᓗᑎᑦ
ᐃᓄᒐᕐᓖᕐᓄᑦ ᐊᐃᔭᐅᓗᑎᑦ ᑎᒍᔭᐅᔪᒫᖅᑐᑎᑦ
ᐊᖕᒡᕐᕋᐅᑎᓗᓂᑦ ᓇᓂᔭᐅᔪᓐᓇᐃᑦᑕᓗᑎᑦᓗ."

ᑭᓯᒥ ᑕᐃᒪᐃᐸᒃᑐᑦ ᐊᖕᒡᕐᕋᕆᔭᕋᓂ.

"Tauvani qiaqattanngillutit
inugarullirnut aijaulutit tigujaujumaaqtutit
angirrautilunitit nanijaujunnaillilutillu."

Kisimi taimaippaktut angirrarijarani.

"Don't cry near there or
the little men will come and take you
to their secret hidden lair."

Only in my hometown.

ᐃᒡᓗᒧᑦ ᐃᑎᖅᣰᑐᓂ
ᓯᑕᒪᑦ ᐊᕐᓇᑦ ᐃᒡᓚᒪᔭᒃᑐᑦ ᐃᒃᓯᕙᐸᣰᑐᑎᒃ,
ᐊᑎᒋᒥᒍᑦ ᐊᐅᖅᑲᖅᑐᒃᓴᐅᐸᣰᑐᑎᒃ.
ᖁᕕᐊᓱᒃᣰᑐᖕᒐ, ᐃᖕᒋᑉᐳᖕᒐ.
ᐊᐅᒪᔪᒥᒃ ᓂᕿᒥᒃ, ᑕᒧᐊᓕᖅᐳᖕᒐ.

ᑭᓯᒥ ᑕᐃᒪᐃᑉᐸᒃᑐᑦ ᐊᖕᒋᕐᕋᕆᔭᕋᓂ.

Iglumut itiqłuni
sitamat arnat iglamajaktut iksivablutik,
atigimigut auqaqtuksaublutik.
Quviasukłunga, ingippunga.
Aumajumik niqimik, tamualiqpunga.

Kisimi taimaippaktut angirrarijarani.

Walking into a house
where four laughing women are seated,
maybe a bit of blood on a blouse.
Happily, I take a seat.
Into the raw meat, I feast.

Only in my hometown.

ᓄᑕᖅᑲᑦ ᕿᑎᒃᑐᑦ
ᑕᐅᕙᓂ ᐱᓱᒡᕕᖕᒥ, ᐃᒐᕝᕕᖕᒥ, ᓴᓚᐅᓱᒡᕕᖕᒥ, ᐊᓇᕐᕕᖕᒥ,
ᐊᓐᓄᕌᓄᑦ ᐃᕐᒥᒡᕕᖕᓕᖕᒥ.
ᐃᕐᒥᒃᓴᕆᐊᖃᓕᖅᐳᒍᑦ!

Nutaqqat qitiktut
tauvani pisugvingmi, igavvingmi, salausugvingmi,
anarvingmi, annuraanut irmigvinglingmi.
Irmiksariaqaliqpugut!

Children playing
in the hallway, kitchen, living room, bathroom, laundry.
Time to wash all!

ᐅᔾᔨᖅᑐᖃᑦᑕᕆᑦ ᓇᒧᑦ ᑐᑎᒋᐊᕐᓂᐊᕐᒪᖔᖅᐱᑦ –
ᐹᓪᓚᑐᐃᓐᓇᕆᐊᖃᕋᕕᑦ.

ᑭᓯᒥ ᑕᐃᒪᐃᑉᐸᒃᑐᑦ ᐊᖏᕐᕋᕆᔭᕃᓂ.

Ujjiqtuqattarit namut tutigiarniarmangaaqpit –
paallatuinnariaqaravit.

Kisimi taimaippaktut angirrarijarani.

Always watch where you're stepping —
you might trip and fall.

Only in my hometown.

ᐊᓂᑉᓗᓂ.
ᓯᓚ ᖃᐅᓪᓗᖅᑐᐊᓗᒃ
14-ᓂᒃ ᐅᑉᓗᓂᒃ ᐱᖅᓯᖅᑐᐊᓘᓚᐅᕐᒪᑦ.
ᐳᐊᕆᔭᐅᑎ ᐊᑐᓕᖅᐸᕋ,
ᓴᐱᙱᓪᓗᖓ ᐃᖅᑭᐊᓱᙱᓪᓗᖓ.
ᐃᓕᓐᓂᐊᕐᓇᖅᓯᕗᖅ, ᓴᓇᓐᓇᖅᓯᕗᖅ ᐅᕝᕙᓘᓐᓃᑦ
ᐸᐃᕆᕝᕕᓕᐊᕐᓇᖅᓯᕗᖅ.

ᑭᓯᒥ ᑕᐃᒪᐃᑉᐸᒃᑐᑦ ᐊᖏᕐᕋᕆᔭᕋᓂ.

Anibluni.
Sila qaulluqtualuk
14-nik ublunik piqsiqtualuulaurmat.
Puarrijauti atuliqpara,
sapinngillunga iqiasunngillunga.
Ilinniarnaqsivuq, sananaqsivuq uvvaluunniit
pairivviliarnaqsivuq.

Kisimi taimaippaktut angirrarijarani.

Step outside.
Only white remains
of the fourteen long blizzarding days.
Get out the shovel,
don't fuss or grovel.
Time for school, work or daycare.

Only in my hometown.

ᖃᐅᔨᓴᐅᑦ ᐃᙲᕐᕋᕗᖅ, ᐊᕐᕕᓂᓖᑦ ᐃᑲᕐᕋᑦ ᖃᙳᒋᖅᐳᑦ,
ᑖᖅᓯᕗᖅ, ᐊᖅᓴᕐᓃᑦ ᓯᓚᒥ ᒧᒥᓕᖅᐳᑦ ᑲᔾᔮᕐᓇᖅᐳᖅ.

Qaujisaut ingirravuq, arviniliit ikarrat qaangiqput,
taaqsivuq, aqsarniit silami mumiliqput kajjaarnaqpuq.

Turns the clock, only six hours more,
darkness surrounds bright lights dancing.

ᐅᓂᑉᑳᖅᑐᐊᑦ, ᑕᐅᑐᕐᕉᕐᓇᖅᑐᑦ, ᐃᖅᑲᐅᒪᓇᖅᑐᑦ
ᐃᓅᔪᓐᓃᖅᓯᒪᔪᑦ, ᖁᕕᐊᓱᒃᖢᑎᒃ ᐱᙳᐊᖅᑐᑦ, ᐊᖅᓴᕐᓃᑦ
ᐊᐅᓚᔪᑦ, ᐃᒻᖏᖅᖢᑎᒃ.
ᐊᖅᓴᕐᓃᑦ ᓇᓂᑐᐃᓐᓇᖅ ᑕᑯᔭᐅᔪᓐᓇᖅᑐᑦ,
ᑭᓯᐊᓂ ᒧᒥᖅᑐᑦ ᐅᕙᒻᓂᒃ ᒧᒥᕈᔾᔨᔪᑦ
ᑭᓯᒥ ᑕᐃᒪᐃᑉᐸᒃᑐᑦ ᐊᖏᕐᕋᕆᔭᕋᓂ.

ᓄᓇᒋᔭᕋᓂ
ᓂᕆᐅᓇᖅᑐᑦ ᖁᔭᒋᔭᐅᑦᑎᐊᓲᑦ.

Unipkaaqtuat, tauturruurnaqput, iqqaumanaqtut
inuujunniiqsimajut, quviasukłutik pinnguaqtut, aqsarniit
aulajut, imngiqłutik.
Aqsarniit nanituinnaq takujaujunnaqtut,
kisiani mumiqtut uvamnik mumirujjijut
kisimi taimaippaktut angirrarijarani.

Nunagijarani
niriunaqtut qujagijauttiasuut.

Stories, images, memories
of spirits, playing happily, fluidly, chanting.
The Northern Lights can be seen in many places,
but they dance for me
only in my hometown.

Where I come from
glimpses of hope are always appreciated.

ᐊᒥᖅᑲᖅᐸᒃᑐᒍᑦ ᐃᑲᔪᖅᐸᒃᑐᒍᑦ ᐊᒥᒐᖅᓱᖕᖏᒃᑳᖓᐅᓪᕚᑕ
ᐊᒻᒪᓗ ᐃᑲᔪᖅᑕᐅᕚᒃᑐᒍᑦ ᐃᑲᔪᖅᑕᐅᔭᕆᐊᖃᓕᕌᖕᒪᓪᕚᑕ.
ᐃᓂᒃᓴᖃᖕᖏᒦᑉᐱᑦ ᓯᓂᒡᕕᒃᓴᖃᖕᖏᒦᑉᐱᑦ?
ᓂᕆᒋᑦ! ᓂᕆᒋᑦ! ᓂᕆᒋᑦ!

Amiqqaaqpaktugut ikajuqpaktugut amigaqsinngikkaangapta
ammalu ikajuqtauvaktugut ikajuqtaujariaqaliraangapta.
Iniksaqanngippiit sinigviksaqanngippiit?
Nirigit! Nirigit! Nirigit!

We share in times of plenty
and are helped in times of need.
Need a place to sleep?
Eat! Eat! Eat!

ᖃᑕᙵᑎᒌᓗᒃᑖᕈᓐᓇᖅᑐᒍᑦ
ᑭᓯᒥ ᑕᐃᒫᐃᑉᐸᒃᑐᑦ ᐊᖏᕐᕋᕆᔭᕋᓂ.

Qatanngutigiiluktaarunnaqtugut
kisimi taimaippaktut angirrarijarani.

Everyone could be family
only in my hometown.